The Inside **GUIDE**

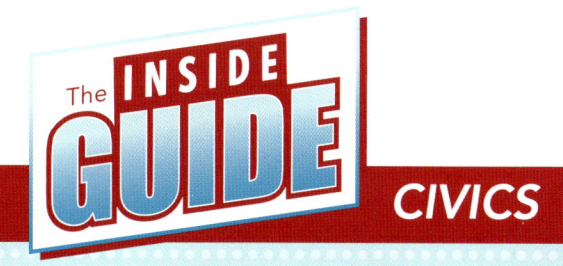

CIVICS

Citizenship

By Cassie M. Lawton

Cavendish Square

New York

Published in 2021 by Cavendish Square Publishing, LLC
243 5th Avenue, Suite 136, New York, NY 10016

Copyright © 2021 by Cavendish Square Publishing, LLC

First Edition

No part of this publication may be reproduced, stored in a retrieval system, or transmitted in any form or by any means—electronic, mechanical, photocopying, recording, or otherwise—without the prior permission of the copyright owner. Request for permission should be addressed to Permissions, Cavendish Square Publishing, 243 5th Avenue, Suite 136, New York, NY 10016. Tel (877) 980-4450; fax (877) 980-4454.

Website: cavendishsq.com

This publication represents the opinions and views of the author based on his or her personal experience, knowledge, and research. The information in this book serves as a general guide only. The author and publisher have used their best efforts in preparing this book and disclaim liability rising directly or indirectly from the use and application of this book.

All websites were available and accurate when this book was sent to press.

Portions of this work were originally authored by Leslie Harper and published as *What Is Citizenship? (Civics Q&A)*. All new material this edition authored by Cassie M. Lawton.

Library of Congress Cataloging-in-Publication Data
Names: Lawton, Cassie M., author.
Title: Citizenship / Cassie M. Lawton.
Description: First edition. | New York : Cavendish Square Publishing, 2021.
| Series: The inside guide: civics | Includes index.
Identifiers: LCCN 2020003283 (print) | LCCN 2020003284 (ebook) | ISBN 9781502656995 (library binding) | ISBN 9781502656971 (paperback) | ISBN 9781502656988 (set) | ISBN 9781502657008 (ebook)
Subjects: LCSH: Citizenship–United States–Juvenile literature. | Immigrants–United States–Juvenile literature.
Classification: LCC JF801 .L38 2021 (print) | LCC JF801 (ebook) | DDC 323.60973–dc23
LC record available at https://lccn.loc.gov/2020003283
LC ebook record available at https://lccn.loc.gov/2020003284

Editor: Kristen Susienka
Copy Editor: Nathan Heidelberger
Designer: Tanya Dellaccio

The photographs in this book are used by permission and through the courtesy of: Cover SAUL LOEB/AFP/Getty Images; p. 4 ozgurdonmaz/iStock/Getty Images Plus/Getty Images; p. 6 monkeybusinessimages/iStock/Getty Images Plus/Getty Images; p. 7 (top) Kim Kelley-Wagner/Shutterstock.com; p. 7 (bottom) SeanPavonePhoto/iStock/Getty Images Plus/Getty Images; p. 8 Lambert/Hulton Fine Art Collection/Getty Images; p. 9 Bettmann/Getty Images; pp. 10, 29 (bottom right) Rawpixel.com/Shutterstock.com; p. 12 brazzo/iStock/Getty Images Plus/Getty Images; p. 13 Dean Drobot/Shutterstock.com; p. 14 LPETTET/iStock/Getty Images Plus/Getty Images; p. 15 KAMIL KRZACZYNSKI/AFP/Getty Images; p. 16 Image Source/Image Source/Getty Images; p. 18 https://upload.wikimedia.org/wikipedia/commons/6/6c/Constitution_of_the_United_States%2C_page_1.jpg; p. 19 Hulton Deutsch/Corbis Premium Historical/Getty Images; p. 20 Andrey_Popov/Shutterstock.com; p. 21 REDPIXEL.PL/Shutterstock.com; p. 22 photosindia/Getty Images; p. 24 Pressmaster/Shutterstock.com; p. 26 Prostock-studio/Shutterstock.com; p. 27 eldadcarin/iStock/Getty Images Plus/Getty Images; p. 28 (top) Library of Congress/Corbis Historical/Getty Images; p. 28 (middle) Archive Photos/Getty Images; p. 28 (bottom) Pamela Au/Shutterstock.com; p. 29 (top left) Everett Historical/Shutterstock.com; p. 29 (top right) Stock Montage/Archive Photos/Getty Images; p. 29 (bottom left) JEWEL SAMAD/AFP/Getty Images.

Some of the images in this book illustrate individuals who are models. The depictions do not imply actual situations or events.

CPSIA compliance information: Batch #CS20CSQ. For further information contact Cavendish Square Publishing LLC, New York, New York, at 1-877-980-4450.

Printed in the United States of America

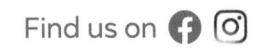

Find us on

CONTENTS

Chapter One: 5
    What's a Citizen?

Chapter Two: 11
    All Different People

Chapter Three: 17
    A Citizen's Rights and Responsibilities

Chapter Four: 23
    Model Citizenship

Timeline: 28
    Key Times in US Citizenship History

Think About It!   29

Glossary   30

Find Out More   31

Index   32

Citizens fill the streets of cities such as New York City.

WHAT'S A CITIZEN?

Chapter One

A country is nothing without the people who live in it. Those people who officially live in a country's cities and towns are called citizens. A person can become a citizen in different ways. Citizens also have certain rights and responsibilities. When people act as good citizens, it's easier for everyone to get along.

Becoming a Citizen

There are two ways to become a citizen of the United States. First, a person can be born a citizen. Anyone born in the United States or a US territory is a US citizen, and anyone born to parents who are US citizens is a citizen. The second way to become a citizen is by law, through a process called naturalization. A person who's born in another country and becomes a US citizen by law is called a naturalized citizen.

Before they become a naturalized citizen, a person has to meet different requirements. They must be 18 years old or older, have to

Fast Fact

Every year, the United States accepts a number of **refugees** into the country. These people find jobs and join a new community. Many eventually become citizens.

have lived in the United States for 5 years (or 3 years if they're married to a US citizen), and have to have learned about US history through several classes. They also have to go to a courtroom and make a promise, called an oath, to the United States. Usually, people who go through the naturalization process are immigrants, or people born in another country who later move to the United States for school, work, or marriage.

Fast Fact

Americans celebrate their country on July 4, or Independence Day. It's also a day many people think about what US citizenship means to them.

US citizens celebrate patriotic holidays, such as Independence Day.

Immigrants

The United States is often called a nation of immigrants. That's because so many immigrants and people **descended** from immigrants call the United States home. This started in the 1500s, when Europeans began arriving in what's now the United States. The first permanent European settlement in today's United States was created in 1565 by the Spanish at St. Augustine in what's now Florida. In 1607, English settlers arrived and started what became the colony of Virginia. A few years later, in 1620, more people from England arrived in what's now known as Massachusetts. These immigrants were called Pilgrims. They set up communities and made connections with Native Americans, who were the only people living in America before Europeans arrived.

Shown here is a group of immigrants taking their oath to become American citizens.

As the years went on, more Europeans came to America, and people from other parts of the world came too. They often came to build a better life for themselves and their families. Your family may have come to the United States hundreds of years ago, or they might have come in just the last few years.

St. Augustine, Florida

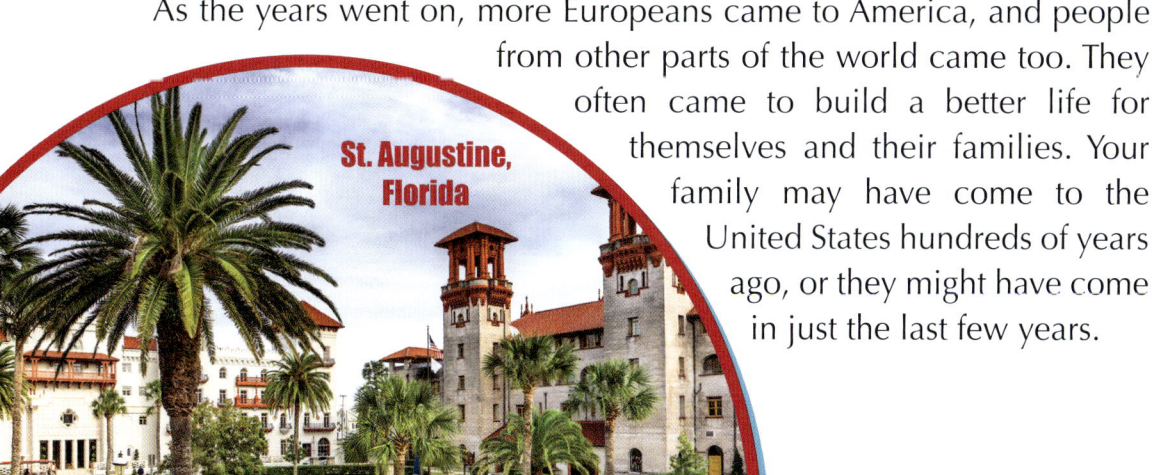

Fast Fact

The Pilgrims came to America on a ship called the *Mayflower*. They traveled to America to practice their religion freely.

Shown here are the Pilgrims, who were some of the first European settlers to call America home.

Today, immigrants continue to come to America. People either come here alone or with their families. Some immigrants flee from dangerous situations in their home countries. They're called refugees. They all want a chance to live a better life in America.

ELLIS ISLAND

In the late 1800s and early 1900s, many families and individuals took boats to get to America. At first, different states kept track of new immigrants, rather than the US government. New York State's center of immigration was Castle Garden in New York City. It operated from 1855 to 1890. In 1892, the US government opened an immigration station (or center) on Ellis Island in New York Harbor. This became the first place many immigrants would stop before continuing to **mainland** America. Usually, poorer families would have to go through Ellis Island. Richer people were processed, or checked, on their ships. From 1892 to 1954, more than 12 million immigrants passed through Ellis Island. Today, it's an important place for tourists to visit and remember the past.

Shown here are immigrants arriving at Ellis Island in the early 20th century.

Many different people call the United States home.

ALL DIFFERENT PEOPLE

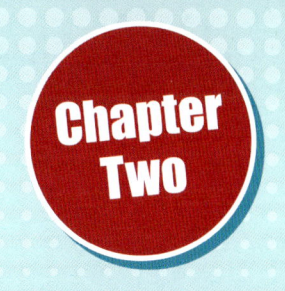

Chapter Two

America is sometimes called a "melting pot." That means many different people from different backgrounds help make up America's population. Most of the people living in the United States are citizens, while others are working to become citizens or aren't planning to stay in America forever. They help make the United States such a **diverse** nation.

Residents

Not all people who live in a country are citizens of that country. Those who aren't citizens are called residents. Residents may not have been born in the country, or they don't have parents who were born there. Residents must go through the naturalization process if they want to become US citizens. If they were a resident in another country and wanted to become a citizen of that country, however, the rules might be different.

Another word sometimes used for a resident is an "alien." Many residents who live in the United States are here legally. They have a **resident card** that gives them permission to live and work in the United States. They come from places around the world, sometimes for a short time, other times for many years. They may also own property. They have many of the same rights as citizens.

A permanent resident card, shown here, is often called a Green Card.

Fast Fact
As of 2020, nearly 330 million people live in the United States.

However, some residents are living in the United States illegally. They don't have the documents needed to live and work in the country, so they're often called undocumented immigrants. If the government catches them, they may be **deported**.

International Students

Many students come to the United States from other countries to go to college. They're called international students, and they're important to the country's education system.

Any international student studying in the United States must apply for the opportunity to study, like every other student. They also need a **visa** or

waiver to enter the United States. There are many international students at US colleges and universities today. They come from places like the United Kingdom, Africa, Australia, the Middle East, and China. Some international students get jobs in the United States after graduating and later become citizens, while others graduate from their schools and go back to their home countries.

Many of America's universities have international students.

Natural-Born Citizens

People born in the United States are called natural-born citizens. That means there's nothing that they must do to become citizens. If one or both of a child's parents are US citizens, then that child is a natural-born US citizen too. This is true even if the child is born while their parents are in another country.

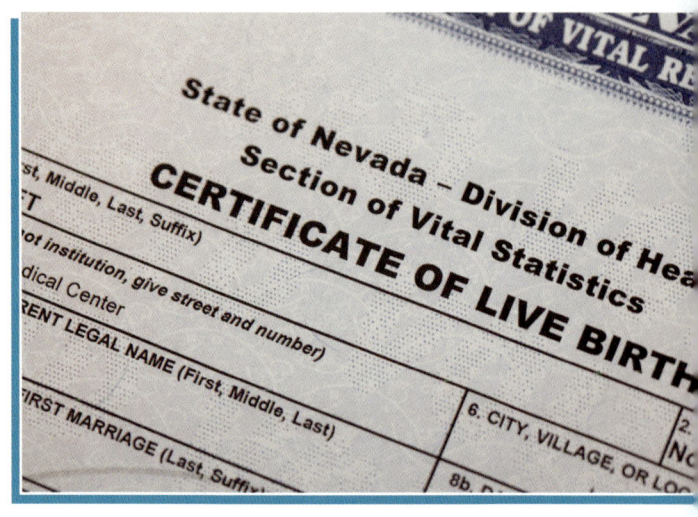

Children born in the United States are automatically US citizens.

Naturalized Citizenship

A naturalized citizen is someone who wasn't born a US citizen but becomes one by law. It takes many steps to become a citizen. For example, a person must show that they know how to speak, read, and write in English. They must also take a test to prove they know about important events in US history and understand how the US government works. After that, a ceremony takes place to welcome new citizens of the United States.

Becoming a naturalized citizen isn't easy. However, many people do it because they want to take part in the rights and responsibilities of their new country, which is what citizenship is all about.

Fast Fact

The United States is one of only a few countries to allow all children born on its soil to be citizens. This is called birthright citizenship.

THE NATURALIZATION CEREMONY

A naturalization ceremony is an exciting event for new citizens and their families. At the ceremony, everyone gathers together. They return their resident cards and then take an oath of allegiance to the United States. In the oath, each person promises to live the life of a good, responsible citizen. The new citizens are given a copy of the US Constitution and a small American flag.

After the person becomes a citizen, they may register to vote in elections, apply for a US **passport**, and apply for **Social Security** benefits. The naturalization ceremony is often celebrated with friends, family, and other important people in the naturalized citizen's life. There might be a smaller, more private party at the person's home later. Becoming a citizen takes a lot of hard work, and it deserves to be celebrated!

Fast Fact

In most cases, naturalized citizens have all of the same rights as natural-born citizens. However, natural-born citizens have one special right. The US Constitution says that a person must be a natural-born citizen to become the president of the United States.

Many immigrants become naturalized citizens every year.

The key to good citizenship is following rules and being responsible for our actions.

A CITIZEN'S RIGHTS AND RESPONSIBILITIES

Chapter Three

There are many important aspects of citizenship. Two of the most important are rights and responsibilities. A right is something that a person is able to do, such as vote or speak freely. A responsibility is something that a person should do, such as helping others. Many rights that have been granted to American citizens can be found in a document called the Bill of Rights. This is a list of the first 10 amendments, or changes, to the US Constitution. In the United States, residents have most of the same rights and responsibilities as US citizens, but some rights, such as the right to vote in US elections, are for citizens only.

Rights

Important rights that citizens of the United States have include the right to assemble, or gather together peacefully in groups. Citizens can also practice any religion they want or no religion at all. They can speak their minds because they have the right to freedom of speech. They can also **protest** to call attention to important issues, such as **climate change** or equal pay between men and women in workplaces. All citizens also have the right to a trial if they get in trouble with the law.

THE BILL OF RIGHTS

The Bill of Rights was added to the US Constitution in 1791. This was only a few years after America won its war for independence from Great Britain in 1783. Initially, the US Constitution, created in 1787, was thought to be all that was needed for US citizens to live life well in the new country. It was quickly discovered, though, that people wanted their rights spelled out. There were many people involved in the ideas behind the Bill of Rights. However, the person who wrote them down was James Madison. He came up with 17 different changes to the Constitution. Eventually, only 10 were accepted and became the Bill of Rights. Today, the Bill of Rights is an important part of US law.

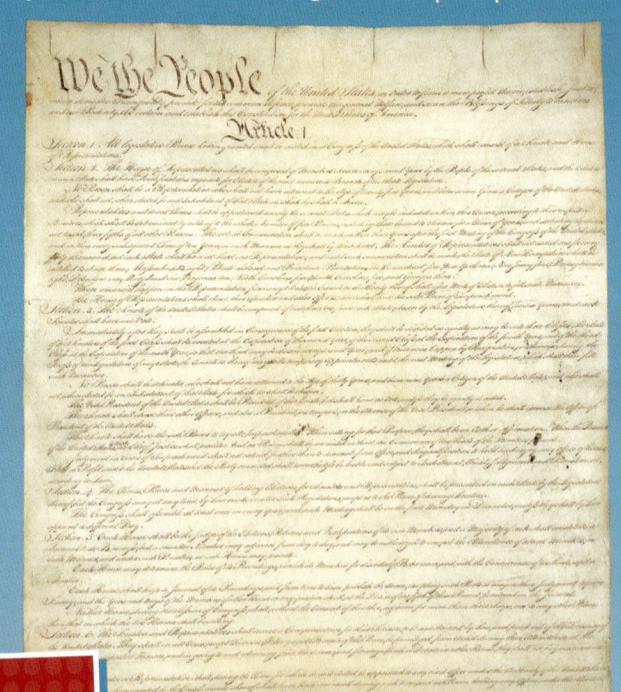

Fast Fact

The writers of the US Constitution are called the Founding Fathers or the Framers. That's because they helped found, or start, America, and they helped frame, or outline, the US government.

The US Constitution is shown here. Many people worked together to create this document.

Many of these rights are part of the US Constitution and the Bill of Rights. However, individual states and cities also have their own laws that grant citizens other rights and give them other responsibilities as well.

Responsibilities

Citizens also have important responsibilities to their country. Responsibilities are things that people must do for the country to keep it running well. For example, all citizens—even kids—have a responsibility to obey the laws of their country, state, and local community. If they don't follow those laws, they might have to pay a fine or even go to jail. It's good for all citizens to know the laws so they can follow them.

One of the most important responsibilities that natural-born or naturalized US citizens have is voting. While it's also a right, some people choose not to exercise it. Those natural-born or naturalized citizens who

Martin Luther King Jr. (*shown here*) fought for equal rights for African Americans.

Fast Fact

For a long time, African Americans didn't have the same rights as white Americans. In the 1950s and 1960s, leaders like Martin Luther King Jr. fought for African Americans to have equal rights. This movement was called the civil rights movement.

are 18 years old and older can vote. There are different elections to vote in for leaders on the national, state, and local levels. Citizens who can vote should vote whenever they can.

Voting is a right and a responsibility.

Fast Fact
Many citizens vote in presidential elections, which choose the next US president. They take place every four years in November.

Male citizens also have a responsibility to serve in the military if they're asked to by the government. This is called a draft. It was needed at certain times throughout history, such as during the **Vietnam War**, but it hasn't been needed in recent years. Still, all men are expected to register their names for a possible draft when they turn 18. (Women don't have to register as of 2020.) The Selective Services System creates a list of all men 18 to 25 years old who register their names. If ever needed, this list would be used to raise more troops for the US military.

Paying taxes is a very important responsibility. Tax money helps the government provide firefighters, police officers, public schools, and many other important things. It's the responsibility of every US citizen and resident to file their taxes every year.

Adults must pay taxes.

Many people in America come from other countries.

MODEL CITIZENSHIP

Chapter Four

One of the best parts about America is its diversity. The men and women who make up the country are unique, or special. Everyone in America can learn from each other. Immigrants and naturalized citizens can teach natural-born citizens about the parts of the world they come from. They can help them understand different **cultures** better.

Sharing Cultures

For hundreds of years, immigrants from Ireland, China, Italy, Mexico, and many other countries all over the world have brought their cultures to the United States. Music, food, art, and language have all been touched by immigration. As new citizens continue to come into the United States, the country's culture will continue to grow and change.

There's no one definition of an "American." Americans come from many different backgrounds, hold many different beliefs, and have gone through many different experiences.

Fast Fact
More immigrants living in the United States today come from Mexico than from any other country.

23

They also might speak differently depending on where in the country they live or where they were born. This is why it's important to treat all people with respect. Being a good citizen means respecting people who are like you and people who are different from you.

Kindness is one of the most important parts of being a good citizen.

What Can You Do?

You might be wondering what else you can do now to be a good citizen. While you might not be old enough to vote or serve in the military, you can do a lot to help the people around you. For example, volunteering is a great way to help others. There are lots of places that need volunteers. Start first with your community. Volunteer to clean up litter, or see if there's an organization for refugees or immigrants in your city or town. By volunteering with local organizations, you can meet new and exciting people while helping others. Another idea is to learn a new language. By learning a language other than English, you can help new visitors or residents in America become more comfortable.

You could also make an effort to learn more about the rights and responsibilities that go along with citizenship. For instance, you could talk to local police officers about following the law. You could also consider becoming involved in a club such as the Boy Scouts or Girl Scouts of America. These groups teach young people the skills needed to be helpful members of society.

Fast Fact
Almost 45 million people living in the United States today were born in another country.

Another way to help in your community is to encourage adults to vote. You'd be surprised how many people might not want to vote. It's important that everyone take advantage of their right to vote, since others worked so hard to get it. You can help others now by learning about the candidates in an election, making posters in support of a candidate, and talking to adults about the candidates. When you can vote, make sure you keep learning about the candidates to make the best decision for yourself.

Whatever else you decide to do, always be kind and helpful. Those are good ways to let others know you're a responsible and **conscientious** citizen. To be model citizens, people must help each other exercise their rights and understand their responsibilities. Teamwork helps make a country a successful one!

Volunteering is an important part of being an active and responsible citizen.

Fast Fact
Many political candidates have social media sites where people can contact them. With a parent or guardian's permission, you can contact candidates to learn more about them and their beliefs.

DUAL CITIZENSHIP

Sometimes, people who gain US citizenship also have citizenship in the country where they were born. This is called dual citizenship. People from other countries who marry US citizens can gain dual citizenship if they become a US citizen. A US citizen married to someone from another country can also work to get dual citizenship in that other country. Dual citizens have different passports for each country. Having dual citizenship makes it easier for families to travel together between two countries regularly. This helps if the family has relatives in both countries.

Shown here are two passports someone might have if they have dual citizenship.

TIMELINE

Key Times in US Citizenship History

1783
The American Revolution between the United States and Britain officially ends.

1868
All African Americans are recognized as US citizens.

1892
Ellis Island opens as the first US government-run immigration center.

1907
Over 1 million immigrants pass through Ellis Island in a single year.

1920
All women are given the right to vote as citizens of the United States.

1954
The last immigrant passes through Ellis Island's doors.

2003
US Customs and Border Protection becomes the main immigration force in America.

THINK ABOUT IT!

1. Why are immigrants important to America's story? What do you think it's like to be an immigrant today?

2. Imagine being one of the first settlers in America. What do you think life was like? How would you feel?

3. Why are there rules to become a citizen if you aren't born in the United States? Do you think the rules are fair? Why or why not? What would you change about the rules if you could?

4. How can you be a model citizen today? What ways can you get involved in your community?

29

GLOSSARY

climate change: The process by which the world's weather patterns are shifting due to human actions.

conscientious: Aware and careful.

culture: The beliefs, practices, and ways of life of a group of people.

deport: To make someone leave a country.

descend: To come from a family line.

diverse: Different; made up of many backgrounds.

mainland: The land on which the majority of the United States rests.

passport: A document that shows a person's country of origin.

protest: To voice opinions publicly.

refugee: A person who comes to live in another country due to difficulties like war or crime in their home country.

resident card: Also called a Green Card in the United States, a document that gives an immigrant permission to live in a country.

Social Security: A US program that provides money each month to the elderly and people who are disabled.

Vietnam War: A war fought between North Vietnam and its allies and South Vietnam and its allies, including the United States, from the 1950s to the 1970s.

visa: A document that allows a person from another country to live and travel in a different country.

waiver: An agreement with certain countries to allow people to enter the United States for a certain amount of time without a visa.

FIND OUT MORE

Books

Carney, Elizabeth. *Ellis Island*. Washington, DC: National Geographic, 2016.

Eggers, Dave. *What Can a Citizen Do?* San Francisco, CA: Chronicle, 2018.

Kreisman, Rachel. *Being a Good Citizen*. South Egremont, MA: Red Chair Press, 2016.

Websites

History: US Immigration Timeline
www.history.com/topics/immigration/immigration-united-states-timeline
This timeline goes through different parts of history and what immigration looked like at key points.

Kids Academy: Good Citizenship
www.youtube.com/watch?v=LKCtzuvBZPc
This video explores what it means to be a good citizen today.

US Citizenship
www.uscis.gov/us-citizenship
This website provides information on what it means to be a US citizen and how to get citizenship in the country.

Publisher's note to educators and parents: Our editors have carefully reviewed these websites to ensure that they are suitable for students. Many websites change frequently, however, and we cannot guarantee that a site's future contents will continue to meet our high standards of quality and educational value. Be advised that students should be closely supervised whenever they access the Internet.

INDEX

A
assembly, right to, 17

B
Bill of Rights, 17–19
birthright citizenship, 5, 14

C
civil rights movement, 19
Constitution, US, 15, 17–19
culture, 23

D
deportation, 12
draft, 20–21
dual citizenship, 27

E
Ellis Island, 9

I
immigrants, 6–8, 9, 15, 23, 25
international students, 12–13

M
marriage, 6, 27
military service, 20–21

N
Native Americans, 7
natural-born citizens, 5, 14, 15, 19–20, 23
naturalization, 5–6, 11, 14, 15, 19–20, 23
naturalization ceremony, 14, 15

O
oath, 6, 7, 15

P
passport, 15, 27
Pilgrims, 7, 8
president, 15, 20
protest, 17

R
refugees, 5, 8, 25
religion, freedom of, 8, 17
resident cards, 11, 12, 15
residents, 11–12, 17, 21, 25
responsibilities, 5, 14, 17, 19–21, 25, 26
rights, 5, 11, 14, 15, 17–19, 20, 25, 26

S
Social Security, 15
speech, freedom of, 17

T
taxes, 21
trial, 17

U
undocumented immigrants, 12

V
visa, 12–13
volunteering, 25, 26
voting, 15, 17, 19–20, 25

W
waiver, 13

32